Mallory's Super Sleepover

by Laurie Friedman

illustrations by Jennifer Kalis

darbycreek

MINNEAPOLIS

CONTENTS

Mallory's SupeR SleepoveR

For Adam and Becca
Love, Mommy

And special thanks to sleepover experts,
Joeli, Grace, and Jordan
—L.B.F.

For Moira, for all of her support, advice,
and encouragement
—J.K.

A WORD FROM MALLORY

My name is Mallory McDonald, like the restaurant, but no relation, and I'm turning ten. Actually, I already turned ten. But I don't feel like I turned ten because I didn't do anything to celebrate.

You're probably wondering why I would let such an important birthday pass without a celebration, and the answer is simple: I couldn't decide how to celebrate.

It wasn't that I didn't try to figure it out. My best friend, Mary Ann, and I made lists of different kinds of parties. We thought about a skating party, a dance party, an art party, a movie party, a costume party, a surprise party, and a games party. We even thought about a *Fashion Fran* party. But none of those parties seemed quite right. It wasn't until this morning during math that we thought up the perfect party . . . a sleepover party!

Of course our teacher, Mr. Knight, wasn't too happy that we were talking about invites vs. evites when we should have been talking about decimals and fractions.

But as soon as we thought of having a sleepover, we knew how much fun it would be. We even came up with a name for it. *Mallory's Super Sleepover.*

I can't wait to plan all the details. There are only two things I need to do first.

Thing #1: Make sure it's OK with my parents. That won't be too hard. I think my parents will be just as excited about this sleepover as I am.

Thing #2: Try to stay calm. But that will be close to impossible because I'm already super excited for what I know will be the most super sleepover tenth birthday celebration ever!

A FAMILY MEETING

"Everyone in the den," shouts Dad. "Time for a family meeting."

I scoop up my cat, Cheeseburger, from my bed and follow my brother, Max, down the hall. Sometimes, actually not that often, I think my parents are mind readers, and today is one of those times.

I was going to call a meeting myself so I could ask my parents about having a sleepover party, and now my parents have gone and called one before I even had to. I'm not sure why they want Max to be part of the meeting. I guess they sensed what I wanted to talk about and they want to make sure everyone in my family does everything they can to make my birthday celebration extra special. Just thinking about it makes me smile.

When I walk into the den, Mom is sitting in a chair. She has a serious look on her face. Dad is standing up with his arms crossed across his chest. He has a serious look on his face too. I think I know why both of my parents look the way they do.

Planning the perfect party is a serious business!

I can just imagine what Dad is going to say about it.

"Family, as you all know, Mallory never got the birthday celebration she deserved. A girl only has one tenth birthday, and we all need to pull together as a family to make this one extra special for her."

I sit down on the couch next to Max.

Deciding how to celebrate your tenth birthday is a V.I.D. (that's short for *Very Important Decision*), and I think I made a good one. Now that I've started thinking about my sleepover, I can't stop. I pull Cheeseburger into my lap and stroke her fur. I try to look calm, but I'm so excited to hear what Dad has to say that I feel like I'm a balloon with too much air in it. If he doesn't start talking soon, I'm going to pop.

The good news is that I don't have to wait for too long.

"Max, Mallory," Dad says in a tone that is every bit as serious as the look on his face.

"Mom and I need to talk to you about something important."

I know what that something important is . . . MY TENTH BIRTHDAY! I send a message from my brain to my mouth not to smile. I want to look surprised and happy when Dad brings it up.

But what Dad brings up doesn't include the words *my* or *tenth* or *birthday*. It includes the words *doing* and *your* and *chores*.

"Max and Mallory." Dad says our names like he wants to make sure we are both listening. "Mom and I are upset about some of the behaviors that are going on around here. Neither of you have been doing a good job lately with your chores."

Dad turns his attention to my brother. "Max, your room is a mess. There are clothes all over the place, and your bed hasn't been made. You forgot to take the trash out last night, and you still haven't swept the garage, which I asked you to do last weekend."

Dad looks at me. "Mallory, your room is a mess too. You need to make your bed and straighten up your closet and your drawers. You left your breakfast dishes on the counter this morning, and Cheeseburger's litter box needs to be changed."

Dad stops talking and looks at my brother and me like it's our turn to say something.

My brother looks at his baseball bag like he wishes he was on the field instead of in our living room. I focus on Cheeseburger. I'd much rather be looking at a cute cat than a mad dad.

Cute cat vs. mad dad
You pick!

Dad nods in Max's direction like he's the oldest so he has to go first.

"I'm sorry," says Max. "When I get home from baseball practice, I promise I'll do all of my chores, and I'll be sure to do them from now on."

Dad nods like he's satisfied with my brother's answer.

Even though doing chores isn't my favorite thing, I know I have to do them too. I also know that if I want to have a sleepover party, now is not the time to argue with Mom and Dad about anything.

I raise my right hand like I'm in a courtroom and about to take an important oath. "I, Mallory McDonald, do officially promise to do all of my chores starting immediately. I also officially apologize for not doing my chores in the past and officially swear I will spend the rest of my life doing any chores that need to be done at 17 Wish Pond Road."

Mom and Dad smile at each other like even though we're having a serious talk, they thought my answer was funny.

Max looks relieved, like he's glad my parents are smiling. "Mom, Dad, I really am sorry about not helping out. I promise I'll try harder. Can I go to baseball now?"

Dad nods like Max is excused.

Max grabs his bag and heads for the front door.

I don't want to be the only kid left to deal with my parents. "Can I be excused too?" I ask. "I want to start cleaning up my room, and I promise I'll change the litter box."

Mom and Dad tell me I'm free to go.

I scoop up my cat and head for my room. I've got a bed to make and drawers to straighten and a litter box to change.

I also have a phone call to make.

The family meeting was not at all what I expected. The word *sleepover* wasn't even mentioned.

I want to ask my parents about having a sleepover, but before I talk to them, there's someone else I need to talk to.

Her name starts with an *M* and ends with an A-R-Y-A-N-N. She's not only my lifelong best friend, but she's also an expert on knowing how to get parents to say *yes*.

A MALLORY MEETING

The family meeting that Dad called didn't exactly go the way I was hoping it would, so I decide to call a meeting of my own.

Actually, I didn't decide that myself. Mary Ann helped.

She convinced me that the only way I would get to have a sleepover is if I show my parents why having a sleepover is a good idea.

I take the piece of paper I've been working on all day off my desk, fold it neatly, and slip it into my pajama pocket.

It's time for some before-bed show and tell.

I go over the plan in my head that Mary Ann and I came up with.

Step 1: When Mom and Dad are already in bed, go upstairs in my *I LUV U* pajamas and pink heart slippers, knock softly on their door, and ask politely if I can come in and talk to them.

Step 2: Show them all the reasons why having a sleepover birthday party is a good idea and tell them how much I really, really, really want to have a sleepover birthday party.

Step 3: Wait for them to say *YES!*

I look in my bathroom mirror

and adjust the ponytail on top of my head. "Wish me luck," I say to Cheeseburger.

I take a deep breath as I walk up the stairs. When I get to Mom and Dad's room, I put *Step 1* into place. I knock on their door. "May I come in please," I ask in my super polite voice.

"Mallory?" Mom says like it's a surprise to hear from me at this hour but a nice one.

I take that as a good sign.

When I walk into their room, my parents are reading in bed.

Time for *Step 2*. I plop down on their bed between them. "Mom, Dad, I have something to show you," I say with a smile. I cross my toes inside my slippers. I hope this goes the way I want it to. I pull the piece of paper out of my pajama pocket and start reading.

10 Reasons Why I, Mallory McDonald, Want to Have a Sleepover Birthday Party and Think It Is a <u>Good</u> Idea

<u>Reason #1</u>: It will be fun for the kids. (They will like doing all the activities.)

<u>Reason #2</u>: It will be fun for the parents. (You like tucking kids in, and you will have lots of kids to tuck in.)

<u>Reason #3</u>: There won't be any unmade beds in the morning. (We will all be sleeping in sleeping bags.)

<u>Reason #4</u>: If a burglar comes to our house, there will be lots of people to scare him away.

<u>Reason #5</u>: If the phone rings, there will be lots of people to answer it.

<u>Reason #6</u>: If something spills, there will be lots of people to clean it up.

Reason # 7 : Having a 10th birthday celebration will make me feel like I'm 10, which will probably make me act like I'm 10. (Fact: 10-year-olds act more mature than 9-year-olds.)

Reason # 8 : Since it is a birthday celebration, we will have birthday cake. You and Dad love birthday cake, and I will make sure you get extra-big pieces.

Reason # 9 : We can roast marshmallows in the backyard. You and Dad love roasted marshmallows (even more than birthday cake).

Reason # 10: It will make me really, really, really happy (so happy that probably all I will ever want to do once the sleepover is over are my chores).

When I finish reading, I put one arm around Mom and the other around Dad. "Please, please, please," I say. "Can I please I have a sleepover party?" I ask in my *this-is-something-I-really-want-and-I-really-hope-you'll-say-yes* voice.

I cross my toes extra hard and make a wish that *Step 3* will happen like it's supposed to.

Mom and Dad look at each other like they're considering my request.

Even though they don't say anything, I think they're having one of those silent *it's-OK-with-me-if-it's-OK-with-you* conversations that parents have when their kids ask for something and they want to make sure they're on the same page before they say *yes.*

"Mallory, a sleepover sounds like a fun way to celebrate your birthday," Mom says like she's the official parent spokesperson.

I uncross my toes and wait for Mom to say what I hope she is about to say next.

"You may have one," she says.

When Mom says that, I feel happiness bubbling up inside me like water in a fountain. I squeeze both of my parents' necks. "Thank you so, so, so much!" My voice sounds as happy as I feel.

Mom unpeels my arm from around her neck and gives me a serious look. "Sleepovers are fun, but they have a way of getting out of hand," she says.

Dad nods like he agrees with Mom. "We want to keep this small. Just a nice night with a few friends."

Mom gives me a serious look like she means what she is about to say next. "Mallory, you have to tell us about all of your plans before you make them, and you have to promise the party will not get out of control."

I don't think either of those things will be hard to do.

I raise my right hand for the second time today. "I, Mallory McDonald, do solemnly swear to tell you about all of my plans before I make them, and I promise I won't let my party get out of control."

Mom and Dad nod like they approve.

I hug them one more time. Then I bound down the stairs. Time to put *Step 4* into place. Email my best friend and tell her the good news!

EMAILS

Even though it's my bedtime, I go straight from Mom and Dad's room to the computer in the kitchen. Some things just can't wait, and telling my best friend, Mary Ann, that my parents said yes to the sleepover is one of those things.

Plus, Mary Ann said she wasn't going to bed until I do.

I flip on the light in the kitchen, sit down at the desk, click on the computer, and log in.

Then I let my fingers do the talking.

Subject: Mallory's Super Sleepover!
From: malgal
To: chatterbox

It worked!

You were right. All I had to do was tell my parents why having a sleepover is a good idea, and they said *yes!*

Yeah! Yeah! Yeah!

I can't wait! I'm so excited! I just have one question: can you come over after school tomorrow so we can start planning?

I can't wait! I'm so excited! (Oops! Did I already say that?) Oh well, I can't wait (oops! sorry for saying it again) for the sleepover and for you to come over after school.

My sleepover birthday will be fun, fun, fun (especially if you help me plan it).

I.H.I.C.U.A.S.T. (That's short for, "*I Hope I C U After School Tomorrow!*")

O.K. Sorry I have to say this one more time . . . I CAN'T WAIT!

Mallory

I click the *send* button and wait.

I hope Mary Ann stayed up like she said she would. I look at the clock on the kitchen wall. I also hope I don't have to wait too long to hear back from her. If Mom and Dad find me on the computer this late, I know I will get in trouble. The last thing I want to do is get in trouble, get punished, and not get to have my sleepover party.

I take a cookie out of the jar on the counter and take a bite.

I try not to look at the clock, but I can't

help it. I watch the second hand go around the face of the clock once, twice, a third time, and a fourth time.

It starts to go around a fifth time, but before it makes it all the way, I hear the three words I've been waiting for: *You've Got Mail.*

I race back to the desk, sit down, and start reading.

Subject: YEAH! YEAH! YEAH!
From: chatterbox
To: malgal

That makes two of us who can't wait! Yeah! Yeah! Yeah!

I'm just as excited as you are about this sleepover. It's going to be so much fun. Of course I'll come over tomorrow after school and help you plan. That is exactly the kind of thing that best friends (especially this best friend) are for.

This is going to be the biggest, bestest (sorry, I know that's not a word, but you know what I mean), superest (same thing here, but you get the picture) sleepover ever.

We should both go straight to bed. We will need our planning sleep (kind of like beauty sleep but different). I'm soooooooooooooo oooooooooooooooooooooooooooooooooooooo excited!

Mary Ann

I smile when I'm done reading and click off the computer. I'm glad Mary Ann is coming over to help me plan. I turn off the light in the kitchen and go to my room.

I get in bed. Even though I'm really happy about getting to have the sleepover, something that Mary Ann wrote in her email is stuck in my head.

I think about what she said about making this sleepover the biggest, bestest, superest sleepover ever. Then I think about what Mom said about making sure this party doesn't get out of hand and what Dad said about a nice night with a few friends.

I don't quite know what Mary Ann has in mind when she says biggest and bestest and superest, but I have a feeling it's not the same thing Mom and Dad have in mind.

I rub Cheeseburger's back. "I'll just have a talk with Mary Ann and tell her what Mom and Dad have in mind," I tell my cat. She purrs like she agrees.

My eyelids are starting to feel heavy, but it's a happy kind of heavy. I close my eyes. I'll talk to Mary Ann tomorrow afternoon, and as soon as I do, we can start planning my sleepover and that will be almost as much fun as having it.

PLANNING TIME

The minute my alarm goes off, I pop out of bed.

Not because it's Monday morning and I can't wait to get to school. Not because I did a great job on my science project and I can't wait to turn it in to my teacher. And not because I have an adorable, new outfit that I can't wait to wear and show my friends.

I can't wait to go to school, because the sooner school begins, the sooner it will end, and the sooner Mary Ann can come over and we can start planning my sleepover party.

Monday afternoon, in my bedroom

Mary Ann plops down on my bed. "I officially call our first *Super Sleepover* meeting to order."

Max sticks his head in my room. "Whatever you two are doing in here, I don't think I like it."

Mary Ann rolls her eyes. "For your information, we're planning Mallory's sleepover party, and you are N.I., which is short for *Not Invited.*"

Max laughs. "I wouldn't want to come anyway."

He closes the door, and Mary Ann opens up a notebook. "The first thing on the agenda is who to invite." She starts reading names from the list she made. "The two of us, April, Pamela, Arielle, Danielle, Hannah, Grace, Zoe, Emma . . ."

I look over Mary Ann's shoulder and start counting names. I stop counting halfway down. I think she's written down every name of every girl we've ever known. Now is definitely the time to have the *my-parents-said-I-have-to-keep-this-party-small* talk with Mary Ann.

When I'm done explaining, Mary Ann frowns. "Haven't you heard the expression *the more the merrier?*" she asks.

I nod. "I have. I'm just not sure my parents have. Why don't we have the two of us plus Pamela and April."

Mary Ann wrinkles her nose like something stinks and it isn't the scent of Max's baseball cleats in the bathroom.

"Mallory, there's a difference between a sleepover and a super sleepover. You can't call your party *Mallory's Super Sleepover* with just four people. We should at least include Emma and Zoe."

She gives me a look like she's an authority on sleepovers and parents "You need to talk to your parents. I'm sure they'll understand when you explain it to them."

Even though I want to do things the way Mom and Dad asked me to, Mary Ann makes a good point. There is a difference between a sleepover and a super sleepover. "I sure hope so."

Mary Ann smiles. "Of course they will. It's your birthday."

Mary Ann makes a check in her notebook. "On to invitations," she says like we're done talking about who to invite and now it's time to figure out how to invite them.

We spend the rest of the afternoon making invitations and party favors and snack lists and activity lists. We plan out our *to-do* schedule for the rest of the week.

Everything sounds like fun, fun, fun, except for the *talking-to-Mom-and-Dad* part. When Mary Ann leaves, I look at our schedule. Unfortunately, the one un-fun part takes place tonight.

Monday night, in the kitchen

"Mallory is everything OK?" asks Mom. "You were awfully quiet during dinner."

I think about this afternoon. Mary Ann and I made a lot of plans for my sleepover.

We planned a cupcake decorating contest and a water balloon fight. We decided that even though Max said he wouldn't want to come to the party, I'm going to see if he wants to invite some friends over for the water balloon fight. Something tells me he'll like that a lot.

Mary Ann and I decided we would tell scary stories while we roast marshmallows

around a fire. We planned what to have
for a midnight snack while we watch a
movie before we go to sleep and what to
eat for breakfast when we wake up. We
even planned to ask our moms if we can
get special matching pajamas.

Even though I know what Mom and Dad
said about small and simple, everything
Mary Ann planned sounds like so much fun.
Just thinking about it all makes me happy.

Dad taps me on the shoulder. "Mallory,
are you in there?" He smiles like he would
love for me to share whatever I'm thinking
about.

"Sorry," I smile like I didn't mean to
be rude. "I was just thinking about my
sleepover."

My parents sit down beside me. "We
want to hear all the details," says Mom.

I take a deep breath. Mary Ann and I

came up with a *how-to-explain-things-to-my-parents* plan. It's time to put it into action.

First, I tell them about our plans.

I tell them about the cupcakes and water balloons and scary stories and even the matching pajamas. Then I show them the invitations we made and tell them how many people I want to invite. I tell them how excited I am for my *Super Sleepover* and that I think this is going to be the best birthday ever. Then I cross my toes and wait. I hope they will be as excited as I am.

Mom and Dad are quiet for a minute. I can't tell if that's a good sign or a bad one.

"Your party sounds a little more elaborate than what we had in mind," says Dad.

I feel like a paper cup of water with a hole in it. I can feel the happiness and excitement draining right out of me.

Mom looks at Dad, then me, like I should cheer up because she's about to give me some good news. "However, Dad and I understand how important a tenth birthday is. You can invite everyone on your list, and the plans are fine."

Then she gets a serious look on her face. "But six girls and water balloons can get out of hand. I expect you and your friends to behave yourselves. No surprises."

I throw my arms around Mom. I can't believe she said yes to everything. "Thanks so much," I tell her. "We'll be good and I promise no surprises."

Mom laughs. "One more thing," she says as I start to walk down the hall to my room.

I stop and turn around. I should have known it was too good to be true.

Mom smiles. "New pajamas sound like fun. I will call Mary Ann's mom and see if she and Mary Ann want to go shopping with us."

I blow my parents good night kisses. So far, so super.

Tuesday afternoon, after school
"I never thought this day would end," I say to Mary Ann as we walk out of the gates of Fern Falls Elementary.

"Now all we have to do is wait," says Mary Ann. "Hopefully Pamela, April, Emma, and Zoe will be some of the first ones out."

But they are not. Mary Ann and I watch as kids start filing through the gates. Some first and second graders. Not who we are waiting for. Some sixth graders. Not who we are waiting for. Arielle and Danielle. Definitely not who we are waiting for. Finally, Pamela walks through the door. Then Zoe. A few more kids leave. Then April and Emma.

"Go!" whispers Mary Ann. She opens the front of my backpack and grabs the envelopes that we addressed yesterday afternoon and shoves them into my hand. I give my friends their invitations and watch as they open them up and start reading.

"I'd love to come!" says Pamela.

You're invited!

to **Mallory's**

10th Birthday Super Sleepover!

Get ready for a super cupcake decorating contest, a super water balloon fight, super snacks, and super scary stories.

When: Friday night, 7 P.M.

Where: Mallory's house

What to wear: favorite PJ's

What to bring: A bathing suit, a sleeping bag, a pillow, and your favorite stuffed animal.

Get ready for some super fun!!
R.S.V.P. to Mallory

"Me too!" says April.

Emma nods like she's in too.

Zoe starts jumping up and down. "Count me in!"

All my friends start talking at the same time.

"What kinds of cupcakes are you going to have?" asks Pamela.

"Can we bring more than one stuffed animal?" asks Emma.

"I love water balloon fights," says Dawn.

"We're going to have so much fun!" squeals April.

That was exactly the reaction I'd been hoping for. I high-five Mary Ann. My sleepover is going to be so super.

Wednesday afternoon, at the mall

"Girls pajamas are up the escalator to your right," a salesclerk tells Mom.

Mary Ann and I follow our moms up the moving stairs.

"I hope they have birthday pajamas," I say to Mary Ann.

We both cross our fingers as we ride up the escalator. "Maybe they will have them with cute little cupcakes all over them," says Mary Ann.

"That would be so cute!" I add.

When we get to the pajama department, Mom and Colleen start looking at one rack, and Mary Ann and I start on another.

"Over here," Colleen says a few minutes later. Her voice sounds excited. When I look, I see why. She's holding up two pairs of pajamas with cupcakes on the front.

Mary Ann and I hug each other.

Our shopping trip is turning out to be just as super as I know my sleepover will be.

Thursday night, on the phone with Mary Ann

"Mallory, it's for you," Max calls from the kitchen.

I run to get the phone.

"It's Birdbrain," he says as he hands me the receiver. "Tell her I've got a very big water balloon waiting for her."

You would think the day before my birthday, he'd try a little harder to be nice to me and to my best friend, but I ignore him and take the phone.

Me: Hey! Hey! Hey!

Mary Ann: Hey! Hey! Hey! I can't believe tomorrow is the big day. Is everything ready?

Me (pulling checklist I made out of my pajama pocket): I think so.

Mary Ann: Snacks and supplies?

Me: Check.

Mary Ann: Marshmallows and movie?

Me: Check.

Mary Ann: Party favors?

Me: Check.

Mary Ann: Did you talk to Max?

Me: He talked to his friends, and they're coming over for the water balloon fight. Everything is a big check.

Mary Ann (laughing): Great. Then get a good night's sleep because you won't get one tomorrow night.

Me (laughing too): Check. I guess we forgot to put sleeping on the checklist.

My best friend and I both laugh as we hang up. My sleepover is going to be so much fun. I've done everything to get ready. Today after school, I even went to the wish pond and made a wish. I wished that my sleepover will be the most super sleepover ever.

Now there's only one thing left to do, and that's wait for it to get here. And the good news is that I don't have to wait much longer.

PARTY TIME

Today is Friday.

Actually, scratch that. Today was Friday. And it was the best Friday ever.

This morning, my family gave me a chocolate chip muffin with a candle in it for breakfast, even though it's not my real birthday. And when I got home from school, everyone in my family helped me get ready for tonight. Mom set up the kitchen for cupcake decorating. Max made sure his friends are coming over for the water balloon fight. Mary Ann helped me make the snack trays for the party. And Dad made a pit in the backyard so we can roast marshmallows while we tell scary stories.

Now it's Friday night, which means it is officially party time.

Even though it's not my official birthday, I scoop up Cheeseburger and sing a little song to myself.

Happy birthday to me.
Happy birthday to me.
Happy birthday, dear Mallory.
Happy birthday to me!

I look at my reflection in the mirror. I don't know if it's my hairstyle or the pajamas Mom bought me for the sleepover, but I think I look older today than I did yesterday.

I smear some sparkly gloss on my lips. I feel older too. Well, I don't know if I really feel older, but what I do feel is ready for my *Super Sleepover* to begin. I look at my watch—6:45. My friends should start arriving in fifteen minutes.

"Mallory, telephone!" I hear Mom calling my name from down the hall.

"Coming!" I yell. I skip down the hall and think about tonight. Just thinking about it makes me happy. I think if I blew my nose right now, the only thing that would come out would be happiness. It sounds gross, but thinking about it makes me laugh.

"Someone looks happy," Mom says when I walk into the kitchen.

Dad plops a birthday hat on my head.

I stick my finger into a bowl of icing and lick it. Then I take the phone from Mom and say hello into the receiver.

I hear a familiar voice on the other end. "Happy birthday, Honey Bee! It's Grandma."

I giggle into the phone. "I know it's you, Grandma. You're the only one who calls me Honey Bee."

"I wouldn't miss the chance to wish you a happy tenth birthday."

"You know it's not really my birthday," I say.

Grandma laughs like she knows and doesn't care. "Your mom tells me you have a big birthday celebration planned for tonight."

I tell Grandma all about my sleepover.

"It sounds like a lot of fun. I wish I could be one of the party guests."

The thought of Grandma in her pj's at my sleepover makes me laugh.

She laughs too. Then Grandma gets quiet for a minute. "Mallory, even though it's not your real birthday, you're celebrating tonight, and I want to tell you about something very important that my mother told me about celebrating a birthday. It's something called birthday magic."

I scratch my head. "It sounds good," I say to Grandma. "But I'm not sure what birthday magic is. Is there a birthday fairy in charge of birthday magic?"

Grandma laughs again. "Birthday magic is something that we all get when we make a birthday wish," she explains. "When you make a wish, birthday magic is what makes it come true."

I scratch my head one more time. I'm not sure that makes much sense.

Your wish is my command.

"Everyone knows that not all birthday wishes come true," I say to Grandma.

"You're right about that," she says. "But here's the secret: birthday magic only works when you wish for something that's really, truly important to you."

I think about the wish I made. I wished that my sleepover will be the most super sleepover ever. "I made my wish," I tell Grandma. "It's really, truly important to me, and I really, truly hope it comes true."

"Honey Bee, I hope whatever it is that you really, truly want and wish for is what you get," she says in the nice grandma voice she always uses when she talks to me.

I hear the doorbell ring. "I think my party guests are starting to arrive," I tell Grandma.

Grandma says *good-bye* and *happy unofficial birthday*.

I hang up the phone and walk toward the door. I think about what Grandma told me about birthday magic. Maybe there is such a thing. There must be, because my party hasn't even started, and I already feel like my wish is coming true.

PARTY CRASHERS

When I open the front door, there are two things standing on the other side of it that I never expected to see.

Thing #1: Arielle

Thing #2: Danielle

They both have on pj's, and they're carrying sleeping bags and pillows. "We heard everyone talking about your sleepover so we figured you must have forgotten to give us our invitations."

Even though today is my birthday and I don't like doing math, I do some anyway. Mallory, Mary Ann, Pamela, April, Emma, and Zoe make six. Now Arielle and Danielle make eight. The last thing I expected at my party was crashers. I know it was the last thing Mom and Dad expected.

They push past me while I'm busy counting. "We'll put our things in your room," says Arielle.

Max shakes his head as they walk down the hall. "Mom's going to kill you," he says.

"Your mom would never kill you, especially not on your birthday," says Mary Ann as she walks inside with her things. She's wearing her cupcake pajamas. Just like I am. She's also wearing a confused look. "What are they doing here?" she asks pointing down the hall.

I quickly explain. "Mom is going to kill me!" I whisper.

Mary Ann pulls my arms out to the sides of my body and puts my thumbs and forefingers together like I'm in a yoga pose. "Breathe deep," she tells me in a calm voice.

"Your mom will understand. Just explain to her that they showed up uninvited."

Mary Ann pushes me toward the kitchen like now is as good a time as any to explain things to Mom. When I walk into the kitchen, Mom is arranging bowls of icing and sprinkles.

She smiles when she sees me. "I heard the doorbell. It's party time!" she says like she's excited for me.

I try to swallow, but I feel like there's a bowl of icing stuck in my throat. Mom and Dad were already so nice about letting me invite so many guests. I don't think they're going to be happy about having two more.

When I finish explaining, Mom purses her lips together like she needs a minute to think before she responds. "There's nothing we can do about it now," she says. "Just make sure they all behave themselves and enjoy your party." Mom puts her arm around me. "It's your party, and I want you to have fun."

I throw my arms around Mom. "Thanks, Mom! You've been so understanding about everything," I tell her.

The doorbell rings again. "Go!" she says. "You're the party girl!"

I run to get the door. This time Pamela and April are on the other side. "Happy birthday, Mallory!" they say.

Zoe and Emma are walking up the sidewalk right behind them. "Happy birthday!" they say too. They all model their pajamas and shove gifts into my arms.

Even though it's not my real birthday, I feel like it is.

"Follow me!" I tell them.

My bedroom looks like a sea of sleeping bags, pillows, stuffed animals, and gifts.

Mom and Dad stick their heads into my room. "Can we come in? We want pictures of all of you in your pajamas."

We all smile and pose while Mom takes pictures. She takes pictures of me with my friends, one of Mary Ann and me in our matching pajamas, and one of me holding Cheeseburger.

"Time for presents!" Mary Ann announces.

Everyone squeals and plops down on my floor and bed as I start opening boxes.

I get a game from Pamela. "It's my favorite," she says.

I get a gift certificate to the mall from April.

Zoe gives me a bunch of bracelets. "I made them myself," she tells me.

Mary Ann gives me a set of ten colors of nail polish. "We can always match, and we have lots of colors to choose from," she says like the present is for both of us.

Mom takes more pictures while I open my presents.

I get some perfume and lip gloss from Emma.

Even Arielle and Danielle give me something. Some really cool, dangly earrings.

"Thanks so much for everything!" I tell my friends.

Mary Ann stands up on my desk chair. "Attention everyone!"

She takes a piece of paper out of her pajama pocket. "We have a busy night ahead of us. First, cupcake decorating in the kitchen. Then we're going to change into our bathing suits for a water balloon

fight vs. Max and his friends. After that, scary stories and roasted marshmallows around the fire. Then movies and midnight snacks."

Everyone claps and cheers like the plans sound great.

And I agree completely. Everything sounds like so much fun. I squeeze Cheeseburger, who is lying beside me. *Mallory's Super Sleepover* has officially begun, and I feel like the wish I made is already coming true. I can't think of one thing that could mess up the most super sleepover ever.

A LITTLE MESS

"Girls, watch me." Mom gives a cupcake icing and decorating demonstration. Then she points to the lineup of bowls along the counter and on the kitchen table and explains how Mallory's Super Sleepover Cupcake Decorating Contest is going to work.

"First, you choose a vanilla or chocolate cupcake. Then you pick your icing." There are bowls of vanilla, chocolate, strawberry, and lemon on the counter.

"Can we use more than one kind of icing?" asks Zoe.

Mom smiles. "I never thought of it," she says. "But I don't see why not."

I picture a four-layer iced cupcake.

chocolate
vanilla
strawberry
lemon

Anatomy of a cupcake

I'm not the only one thinking about the possibilities. Everyone starts talking at the same time. Mom holds up her hand like she's not done and wants everyone's attention. "When you finish icing, it's time to decorate."

She points to the bowls of sprinkles, candy hearts, chocolate chips, silver and gold balls, mini umbrellas, and bottles of squirt icing. "As you can see, you have lots of options. Take your time and be creative."

Mom puts her arm around Crystal, my favorite babysitter who has come to help out for the night. "Mallory's dad and I are going to go on a walk. Crystal is in charge while we're gone. When we come back, we're going to choose the winning cupcake, and then we'll put a candle in it and sing *Happy Birthday* to Mallory."

Everyone looks at me, and I grin.

"OK, girls, time to start decorating," Crystal says.

Mom wishes us luck as she leaves the kitchen.

Everyone grabs cupcakes and knives and gets busy icing cupcakes.

"This is fun," says Emma. She and Mary Ann slather their cupcakes with pink icing. Pamela starts with vanilla. April chooses lemon, and everyone else picks chocolate.

"Icing cupcakes is hard," says Emma.

"Let me show you something," says Crystal. She takes the knife from Emma and shows her how to smooth the icing along the top and edges of the cupcake.

I try to copy what she's doing, but it's not so easy. Little bits of cupcake keep getting in my icing.

"Will you help me?" April asks Crystal.

As soon as Crystal takes the knife from April and starts spreading icing, Crystal's cell phone rings. Crystal puts the knife down. When she looks at her phone, she smiles. "Girls, keep icing. I'll be right back."

I wink at Crystal. I know it's her new boyfriend on the phone. Lately, that's who she's always with on the phone.

April starts icing again, but she looks like she could use some help. There's just as much icing on the kitchen table as there is on her cupcake.

And she's not the only one having trouble. Mary Ann has used so much icing you can't tell where the kitchen table ends and her cupcake begins. Arielle's cupcake falls off the counter. When she picks it up, chocolate icing smears all over the floor. "Oops!" she says like she knows she made a big mess but didn't mean to. Danielle drops her knife, and icing sticks to the counter, the cabinet, and the floor.

"Time to switch," Zoe announces like she liked her idea of using lots of kinds of icing.

Everyone starts passing around the bowls of icing. Pink and yellow and white and brown goo gets all over the counter and table.

Zoe's cupcake is piled so high with icing it falls over. Pamela tries to top her cupcake with gold balls, and it rolls off the table. Danielle and Arielle start laughing.

"Time to decorate," Zoe announces like she's the one in charge of the cupcakes.

Everyone reaches for the bowls of decorations and bottles of squirt icing and starts piling different toppings on the cupcakes.

"This is really fun," laughs Emma as she covers her cupcake with sprinkles.

"Look at mine," says April. Her cupcake looks like a tower of chocolate chips.

Mary Ann covers the edges of her cupcake with red squirt icing and adds silver balls.

A few minutes later, there are as many sprinkles and candy hearts and gold and silver balls and chocolate chips on the floor as there are on the cupcakes. Red and purple and green squirt icing is all over the counter. The kitchen table has so much icing and decorations on it that it looks like a giant cupcake.

Arielle sticks an umbrella in her cupcake and looks at the clock. "I'm done," she says like she's ready for another activity.

Danielle nods like she agrees. "What's next?" she asks.

I look around the kitchen and groan. I need to get Crystal, and we need to clean up this mess. She's not going to be too happy when she sees it, but Mom and Dad are going to be even less happy.

I start to tell my friends that what's next is we need to clean up the kitchen before Mom and Dad get back, but Danielle interrupts me. "Look outside!" she screams.

Everyone runs to the window.

Max and his friends Adam and Dylan are standing beside a huge pile of water balloons.

"We're going to get soaked!" screams Arielle.

"We have to start making balloons," says Danielle.

"To the bathroom!" yells Zoe before I can say anything else.

She and Emma grab a handful of balloons off the counter and run toward my bathroom. April and Pamela grab another handful and follow them. Arielle and Danielle are right behind them. A messy kitchen was bad, but making water balloons in the house is even worse. Water is going to get everywhere.

I turn to Mary Ann and give her a *your-my-best-friend-and-I-could-use-your-help* look. "We have to clean this kitchen up before Mom and Dad get back."

But Mary Ann turns my head so I'm looking at the pile of water balloons in the backyard. "If we don't start making balloons and fast, what Max and his friends are going to do to us is a whole lot worse than what your parents are going to do to us."

Before I can say that I see the big pile of water balloons the boys have made and I also see the big mess in the kitchen, Mary Ann is running down the hall like she wants to do her part to fill up balloons.

I look at the kitchen. I try to wipe some of the icing off the counter, but when I do, it just smears everywhere and makes a bigger mess. I can feel sprinkles sticking to the bottom of my feet. I don't know where to start cleaning.

Even worse, I don't know if I should clean up this mess or try to prevent another one from happening.

A BIG MESS

I wish I had a sign that said *stop filling up water balloons in the house and help me clean up the kitchen.* But even if I did, I don't think anyone would read it. There's a huge stack of water balloons on the floor of my bathroom. My friends are getting ready for battle.

Part of me thinks we should stop and clean up, but the other part of me knows we're going to get soaked if we don't defend ourselves.

I need someone to help me decide which part of me I should listen to. "Maybe we should get Crystal and clean up the kitchen before Mom and Dad get back," I whisper to Mary Ann.

She looks at me like I've lost something and that something is my mind. "We don't have a moment to lose," says Mary Ann.

"We've got to attack when the boys are not expecting us," says Arielle.

"It's all about surprise," says Danielle.

"They think we're in the kitchen decorating cupcakes," Zoe says like she's sure we're going to outsmart the boys.

Maybe my friends are right. "But what about the mess in the kitchen?" I ask Mary Ann.

She ignores my question like the kitchen is not what we need to be thinking about right now. "Bathing suit time!" Mary Ann proclaims.

We all scramble around my room and change into our suits.

"OK," Mary Ann says when everyone is done changing. "It's time for the battle to begin. Remember our strategy: Surprise the boys. Go quietly and hit them hard. Take as many balloons as you can carry."

Everyone starts grabbing balloons. Some of them break while people are grabbing. Zoe drops one on the floor of my bathroom. Emma starts laughing and she drops one too. There are broken balloons and water everywhere. My bathroom looks like a swimming pool.

"C'mon!" Mary Ann whispers. "Let's go!"

Everyone grabs balloons and follows Mary Ann out my door. Pamela drops balloons in my bedroom and so does April.

My room is just as big of a mess as my bathroom.

Balloons drop as my friends walk down the hall toward the living room.

"Maybe I should get Crystal to help us clean some of this up," I say to Mary Ann.

"Quiet!" says Mary Ann like she's more worried about the noise we're making than the balloons we're dropping.

I look at the puddles of water on the floor. I feel like I can see Mom's and Dad's faces reflected in them. I don't see happy faces.

"OK," Mary Ann whispers as we approach the living room. "Ready."

Each girl tries to hold one balloon in her throwing arm and the other ones with her free arm. But my friends aren't very good at this. Balloons start dropping all over the living room floor.

Mary Ann ignores the mess. "Aim," she whispers.

It's my party, and I wish I could focus on the water balloon fight, but my mind keeps thinking about Mom and Dad and what they're going to say when they see this mess. I try to use my now ten-year-old brain to think what I should do.

"Your parents won't be back for a little while," it tells me. *"Go get your babysitter and tell your friends to help you clean up the messes*

in the kitchen and the bathroom and your
bedroom and the hallway and then have the
water balloon fight."

I silently thank my brain.

That's a really good plan. I put my
balloons down. I knock on a coffee table
to get everyone's attention. But when I do,
Mary Ann looks at me like I just gave away
our whereabouts.

"FIRE!" she says in her *you've-blown-our-
cover-so-we-have-no-choice-but-to-attack* voice.

And before I have a chance to ask my
friends for their help, they start running
through the living room to the backyard.
Water balloons start flying. And not all
of them are flying outside. Some of my
friends start throwing their balloons before
they even get out of the living room.

I can't believe what I'm seeing. I pinch
myself to make sure I'm not having a bad

dream, and unfortunately, I'm not.

There's water and broken balloon pieces on the carpet, on the furniture, and dripping down the walls. Even the curtains are wet. When I pictured a water balloon fight, I pictured me having a good time. I pictured it outside in the backyard, not in my house. I never pictured me standing alone in a messy, wet house.

I hear screaming and laughing outside in the backyard. My friends start running back through the house to get more balloons.

Then I hear another sound.

It's not laughter or screaming. I hear the front door open and shut. Then I hear footsteps and talking. It's not kid footsteps or talking. It's adult footsteps and talking.

Then I hear something even worse. My name.

"MALLORY!"

Mom and Dad are in the living room standing in front of me with their arms crossed. Crystal is beside them. I can't decide who looks madder.

All of a sudden, I feel as wet and soggy as the room around me.

My friends run back in the living room with an armload of balloons. When they see Mom and Dad and Crystal, they stop.

"Mallory, what happened?" asks Mom. She looks around the room like nothing I say could possibly explain it.

Before I even have a chance to talk, Mom keeps going. "Mallory, you and your friends were supposed to be in the kitchen decorating cupcakes. The kitchen is a big mess, and there's water and balloons all over the house."

I look at Mary Ann. I am hoping she can do something, give me a sign, anything, to help me out of this mess. And she does. She moves her eyes in Crystal's direction and gives me a *she-was-supposed-to-be-the-one-in-charge* look.

I don't know why I didn't think of that. It's the perfect explanation. I know why Mary Ann is my best friend. She's so smart.

I look at Mom and Dad. "None of this would have happened if Crystal had been doing her job," I say. Then I look at Crystal. "She was outside talking on the phone to her boyfriend."

Crystal looks like she's a puppy who just had an accident in the house and is getting in trouble with her owner.

"Mallory, I shouldn't have been outside, but all you had to do was come and get me."

She makes it sound like I'm the puppy owner and it's my fault the puppy had the accident in the house because I didn't open the door and let her outside. Crystal always looks happy, but not right now. I've never seen her look so upset.

I don't like being the one she's upset with, but I don't know what else I could have said.

Dad clears his throat. "Girls, Mallory's mom and I are not happy about this mess. You're all going to have to help clean up."

Mom goes to the kitchen to get sponges and rags and a mop. Dad walks Crystal to the door. I watch as she leaves. She doesn't even say good-bye.

I'll have to fix things with Crystal later. Right now, I have another mess to clean up. Actually, I have several.

I grab a rag and start scrubbing the floor. The only thing that is a bigger mess than the kitchen and the living room and my bedroom and my bathroom is this sleepover.

I cross my toes.

I sure hope things improve.

A BAD-AS-IT-GETS MESS

Roasted marshmallows always taste good, but they taste even better when you've just scrubbed a kitchen and a living room and a bedroom and a bathroom. That's what my friends and I spent the last hour doing.

I had to promise Mom and Dad no more messes. That promise shouldn't be hard to keep. I didn't like cleaning up and neither did my friends.

"Who wants to hear another scary story?" asks April.

Everyone shudders but in a good way.

"No more stories," Mom says with a smile. She starts collecting our marshmallow-roasting sticks. "You girls have been out here long enough. It's time to go inside. You can watch a movie and have a midnight snack. Then it's bedtime . . . or should I say sleeping-bag time." Mom smiles like she likes her joke.

Everyone giggles as we walk inside. This party is finally becoming what it was supposed to be in the first place . . . fun!

I turn on the movie, and my friends and I all curl up on the couch and on the floor. "Who wants popcorn?" Dad walks in the living room with two big bowls of popcorn and the tray of snacks that Mary Ann and I put together after school.

We eat and watch the movie.

When it's over, Mom and Dad help us clean up the leftover snacks. "Why don't you girls bring your sleeping bags and pillows and stuffed animals in the living room," says Dad. "There's more room, and I think you'll be more comfortable."

"Last one to Mallory's room is a rotten tomato," says Emma.

We all race down the hall to get our stuff.

"You sound like a herd of stampeding buffalo," Max yells from his room.

Some of my friends giggle like they think Max is funny, but Mary Ann and I tell them he's definitely not.

We get our stuff and set everything up in the living room. When we're done, Dad turns out the lights. "Good night, girls," says Mom. "It's lights out time."

Everyone tells Mom and Dad good night as we crawl into our sleeping bags.

When we hear Mom and Dad's door close, Mary Ann and I pull something out of our sleeping bags. "It might be lights out time," whispers Mary Ann. "But we have flashlights!"

Mary Ann and I pass around the stash of flashlights that we hid inside our sleeping bags earlier. We all turn on our flashlights.

"Should we tell more scary stories?" asks Emma.

"We could play Truth or Dare," says Zoe.

Pamela yawns. "I'm sleepy. Maybe we should go to sleep."

Arielle and Danielle shine their flashlight in Pamela's direction. "Go to sleep at your own risk," they say at the same time.

Everyone giggles.

"Shhh! If Mom and Dad hear us, they'll come down and take away the flashlights," I say.

"Does anyone want to hear the story of when I went to visit my grandma's house and my brother and I thought we heard a ghost in the attic?" asks April.

Everyone shivers as April tells us about the strange sounds she and her brother heard coming from her grandmother's attic. Everyone says how scary ghosts are. Everyone except one person and that one person is sound asleep.

Arielle shines her flashlight in Pamela's eyes, but Pamela doesn't move. Arielle and Danielle give each other a thumbs-up sign.

"We hid something in our sleeping bags too," whispers Danielle.

"And it's not flashlights," Arielle adds. She puts her hand over her mouth like she doesn't want to start laughing.

She and Danielle reach into their sleeping bags and and each pull out a bag. I shine my flashlight on it so I can see what they have. It looks like markers. I can't imagine why they would hide markers in their sleeping bags.

But I don't have to wait long to find out.

Arielle and Danielle cross the room quietly to where Pamela is sleeping. Then I see what they are going to do with the markers.

Arielle starts drawing a flower on Pamela's cheek. Danielle draws a bird on her forehead.

"What are you doing?" I whisper.

"Shhh!" says Danielle. "You'll wake her up."

Arielle takes another marker and draws hearts and stars all over Pamela's nose and chin. "We said go to sleep at your own risk," she says.

Danielle draws a tree down one of Pamela's arms. Arielle draws a vine and some leaves down the other one.

Mary Ann giggles. "I'm glad I wasn't the first one to fall asleep."

"Me too," says Emma.

Arielle draws a bird on her shoulder.

I try to swallow, but I feel like there's a bird in my throat. "You have to stop," I whisper to Arielle and Danielle. "Pamela is going to be upset when she wakes up and sees what you're doing."

"She's not going to wake up if you stay quiet," says Arielle.

"She won't care," says Mary Ann like she's taking Arielle and Danielle's side and not mine. "You have to admit it's kind of funny, and they did warn her not to go to sleep." Mary Ann puts her hand over her mouth like she doesn't want to laugh out loud.

Emma and Zoe and April nod like they kind of agree and think it's funny too.

I can't believe Mary Ann is taking Arielle and Danielle's side, and not mine. And I can't believe she and the rest of my friends think this is funny too.

I know Pamela, and I know she's not going to like what Arielle and Danielle are doing to her. I start to say something, but my friends stare at me like they're going to be mad at me if I start talking and wake up Pamela.

I know I should say something, but for

some reason, when I open my mouth,
nothing comes out. I don't know why it's
hard to say what I know I should say. I
open my mouth, to try again. This time,
something comes out, but not words.

"AH-CHOO!"

A huge sneeze comes out, and when
it does, my friends looks at me, and then
they look at Pamela, who rubs her eyes,
and then opens them.

I shine my flashlight in her direction.

Pamela looks confused. "Why is
everyone staring at me?" Then she looks
down at her hands. Even in the dark,
she can see there's something on them.
Pamela looks even more confused. She
gets out of her sleeping bag and walks
down the hall to my room.

We wait for her to come back, but she
doesn't.

"What do you think she's doing?" whispers April after what seems like a very long time.

"She's been back there forever," says Emma.

I don't know what Pamela is doing, but whatever it is, I don't think I like it. "Do you think I should go check on her?" I ask.

But I don't have to check. Someone turns the lights on in the living room. Pamela walks into the living room, and Mom and Dad are with her. I don't know who looks more upset, Pamela or my parents.

The next thing I know, the doorbell rings. Pamela starts picking up her stuff.

"Pamela is very upset by what you girls did to her," Mom says. She puts an arm around Pamela and walks her toward the door. "She called her mother, and she's going home."

Mom and Dad walk outside to talk
to Pamela's mom. I know I need to do
something. I get out of my sleeping bag
and grab a party favor. I walk over to
the door.

I try to give Pamela her party favor.
"Pamela, I'm really sorry." I try to explain
what happened.

But Pamela doesn't want my apology or my explanation or my party favor.

I watch a tear fall across one of the flowers on Pamela's cheek. Pamela's mother takes Pamela's things from her and leads her to her car.

I feel like my *Super Sleepover* just turned into a super mess.

Some messes can be cleaned up with sponges, rags, and a mop, but some messes are much harder to clean up, and I think this is one of those messes.

NIGHTMARE ON WISH POND ROAD

A SUPER SCARY STORY
by Mallory McDonald

(NOTE #1 TO READER: This super scary story was not told at my sleepover. Even scarier ... It happened at my sleepover!)

FOREWORD

Once upon a time, there was a little girl. Actually, she wasn't so little. She was ten, which isn't little at all. Anyway, this girl had a sleepover party to celebrate her tenth birthday. She invited some friends and planned some fun stuff to do, but her  sleepover turned out to be nothing like other sleepovers.

(NOTE #2 TO READER: That was just the background info. We haven't gotten to the super scary part yet.)

Her sleepover was different. It all started in the kitchen. She and her friends were supposed to be neatly decorating cupcakes, but her friends weren't neat cupcake decorators. They made a big mess doing it.

What you don't want your kitchen to look like

Then, before they could clean the mess up, they got into a water balloon fight with the girl's brother and his friends. Water got everywhere. Not just on people and not just outside in the backyard where it should have gotten. But some water got inside the house too.

This all happened while the girl's parents were out taking a walk. It shouldn't have happened because the parents left a babysitter in charge of the kids, but it did, because instead of babysitting (or in this case, kid sitting), the babysitter (or in this case, kid sitter) was busy talking on her cell phone to her boyfriend. You're probably wondering why the girl didn't just go get the sitter when the problems started. Well, a lot of people, like the sitter and the girl's parents, wondered that too.

(NOTE #3 TO READER: You're probably also wondering when this story gets scary. Keep reading!)

When the girl's parents came home, a couple of things happened.

First: They saw the mess.

Second: They got kind of mad. (Actually, a little more than kind of mad, but we won't go into all that here.)

Third: They made the girls clean up everything.

Then something good actually happened: The party continued.

(NOTE #4 TO READER: I bet when you read the part about the party continuing, you decided this story is not bad and certainly not super scary. You were probably thinking that all things considered, it sounded pretty good. But we are getting to the super scary part, I promise.)

The girls did things that most girls do at sleepovers.

They put on their pajamas. They told stories and roasted marshmallows around a fire. They watched a movie and ate late-night snacks.

Then some of the girls did something that most girls probably don't (and shouldn't) do at sleepovers. They decided to decorate (actually, a little more than decorate, but we won't go into all that here) one of the girls who fell asleep early.

When she woke up and saw what they had done, she got so upset that she called her mom and told her she wanted to go home.

(NOTE #5 TO READER: OK. Here's what you've been waiting for. The super scary part is about to begin.)

So she left, and right when she did, the party girl's parents told the party girl they wanted to see her in their room. She didn't really want to go to their room, but she knew she didn't have a choice.

When she got there, her parents looked mad.

The super scary part was that she had never seen her parents look so mad.

It was like all of a sudden they were transformed from nice, normal-looking parents into scary creatures like the kind you see in late-night horror movies.

Their eyes got big.

Their faces turned red.

Their bodies started to shake.

Their teeth looked long and sharp.

Then they started to yell. (If you asked them, they would say they were not yelling. They would say they were talking sternly. But if you ask the girl, she would say that whatever you want to call the way they were talking was even scarier than the way they looked.)

With their mad voices and their mad faces, they told the girl how upset they were with her and some of her choices. They talked in their mad voices and with their mad faces for a very long time. (They talked for so long that the girl began to tremble and shake and wonder if she would ever be OK and happy again and could only hope that her friends who were still downstairs in their sleeping bags and pajamas would send someone up to get her.)

But unfortunately for the girl, no one came to get her. Then, just when it didn't seem like her parents could make her feel any more scared than she already did, they did.

They told the party girl that she was free to go.

(NOTE #6 TO READER: I bet you are thinking that this was good and it made her happy, but it didn't. It made her even more scared, and here is why.)

As the party girl walked down the stairs to join her friends, she knew she had not heard the end of this.

She knew what her parents really meant when they said she was *free to go* was that she was *free to go FOR NOW.*

Even though she had been plenty scared by her parents' scary looks and scary voices, she knew that the scariest part of the story was yet to come.

She crawled into her sleeping bag next to her best friend. Then she rolled over and tried to sleep. But she could not sleep. Something deep inside her ten-year-old body told her that the scariest part of the story would begin in the morning after her friends would all leave.

And she wasn't looking forward to that part of the story at all.

The End. But only for now.

AFTERWORD

One more thing happened when the girl crawled into her sleeping bag next to her best friend. She came to a decision. She decided that all the bad stuff that happened at her sleepover wasn't all her fault. It was her best friend's fault too.

Her best friend was the one who told her to invite a lot of people even though she knew the girl's parents had said to keep things small. She was the one that said to leave the kitchen a mess and to go make water balloons in the house. She was the one who told the girls to throw the balloons. And she was the one who laughed when some of the girls at the party started decorating another girl at the party. She was the one who had not been acting like a best friend.

The more the girl thought about the things her best friend had done, the madder she got. So when her best friend said, "Good night, sleep tight, and don't let the bedbugs bite" (which is what they always say at sleepovers before they go to sleep), the girl looked at her best friend and said, "I hope they bite you." And she told her why.

Then she closed her eyes and pretended to go to sleep. But like I said before, she couldn't sleep because she was scared, and now to top things off, she was mad too.

And to be perfectly honest, a little bit confused.

T-R-O-U-B-L-E!

All of my friends and my brother and my parents are having hot chocolate and French toast for breakfast. That's what I'm having too, except mine is being served with a side order of trouble. I can tell by the way Mom is not looking at me that my side order will be served the minute my friends leave.

And I'm right.

As my friends start to leave, I give out the beaded picture frames that Mary Ann and I made for party favors. When I try to give one to Mary Ann, she shakes her head like she doesn't want it. I know she's mad that I'm mad at her, but I don't see how that gives her the right to be mad at me.

As soon as my last friend walks out the front door, Mom and Dad tell me they want to see me in my room.

"Someone's in T-R-O-U-B-L-E," Max whispers as I walk past him.

I almost never agree with my brother, but this morning, I know he's 100% right.

The minute I get to my room, Dad tells me to sit down.

I sit cross-legged on my bed and look at my parents who are standing up cross-armed. I have never felt so small, and they have never looked so big.

Dad clears his throat. "Mallory, Mom and I are extremely upset with you," he says.

Little helpless child vs. BIG SCARY PARENTS

I look down at my bedspread. "I know," I say in a soft voice.

"We trusted you," says Mom. "And you broke that trust in many ways."

I look down and focus on a spot on my bedspread. I wish I could be that spot and not me right now. I don't know what to say to my parents.

But they seem to know exactly what to say to me.

"Mallory, we are disappointed in you," says Mom. "You asked if you could have a sleepover party, and we said yes. We told you that we expected it to be a nice night with a few friends. We told you that we wanted your help in making sure the party did not get out of hand. When you asked if you could invite more people than we had in mind, we said yes. And when extra friends showed up at the last minute, we very nicely told you we understood and that it was your birthday and it was OK."

Mom starts pulling back fingers as she talks like she's keeping a tally of all the things that I asked for and that they gave to me. "You asked for new pajamas, and we got

you those. You told us what you wanted to do at the party, and we said OK to everything."

Mom recrosses her arms and tucks her hands around her sides like she's done counting because there's no sense in even trying to keep track of all the nice things they did for me.

"Mallory, we did everything we could to make your party exactly what you wanted it to be, and I don't understand how you could have let things get so out of hand." Mom stops talking and looks at me.

Even though I'm glad she's done, at least for the moment, in a way, I wish she'd keep going. I know I did so many things wrong, and I'm not even sure what to say to my parents.

Neither of them says a word. It's my turn to talk, and I know it.

"Mom, Dad, I'm really sorry about everything that happened at the sleepover."

Mom and Dad just look at me like what I said is nice, but it doesn't begin to explain things. I take a deep breath. I know I owe my parents an explanation. I think back to when Mary Ann and I first started planning the party. Even though Mary Ann wanted everything to be big, big, big, I knew Mom and Dad wanted me to keep things small.

"Mallory, we're waiting," says Dad.

I know I don't have a choice. It's time to start explaining.

"I didn't mean for the party to get out of control," I tell Mom and Dad. "When Mary Ann and I first came up with the idea of having a sleepover, it seemed like a good idea. When I talked to you about it, I know you wanted me to plan something small and nice with just a few friends."

I pause. I want to get my words right. "I didn't think that would be hard. But Mary Ann had different ideas. She thought everything needed to be big to be fun. She wanted to invite a lot of people. And once the party started, it was like everything just kind of got out of control."

My lips feel dry, but I keep talking. "I know we shouldn't have made a mess in the kitchen or had the water balloons in the house. I know I should have gone to get Crystal once things started to get out of hand. But Crystal was supposed to be the babysitter and she shouldn't have gone outside to talk on her phone."

My throat feels tight, but I know I have more explaining to do. I tell Mom and Dad that it was Arielle and Danielle's idea to decorate Pamela. "I know they shouldn't have done it, but it was like one thing led to another and before I could stop them, they were laughing, and they just kept doing it."

I think before I say what I'm about to say next. "And the biggest problem is that Mary Ann is my best friend and she didn't help me stop anyone from messing up the kitchen or making water balloons in the house and coloring on Pamela."

Mom and Dad listen to what I have to say. I'd like to see them nod like what I'm saying makes sense or hear them say, *"Sweet Potato, we understand. Growing up isn't easy, and don't worry, we forgive you."*

But that's not what they do or say.

Dad shakes his head like what I've said is not a good explanation. "Mallory, Mom and I agreed to let you have a sleepover. We gave you a few simple rules that we expected you to follow, and you didn't do that."

Dad pauses like he wants every word that he's saying to sink into my brain. "You listened to what Mary Ann and your other friends wanted you to do instead of doing what you knew was the right thing to do."

Mom picks up where Dad leaves off. "Mallory, it's not Mary Ann's fault that she thought having a big party would make it fun. It was your fault for not explaining to her that your parents said you had to keep the party small. She and the rest of your friends should have known better than to make a mess in the house or color on someone. Crystal shouldn't have been outside on the phone, but this is your house and it was up to you to go get her and to stop your friends when things started going wrong."

I nod, like I understand what Mom is saying.

But she keeps explaining like she's not sure I do. "Part of growing up is taking responsibility for your actions and thinking through the consequences of your choices. Just because your friends do something or tell you to do something, does that make it right?"

Mom looks at me like she's waiting for an answer.

"Mallory, as you get older, there will be lots of things your friends might do, and just because they think it's a good idea or it might be fun, are you going to do those things if you know they're the wrong things to do?"

I think about some of the things I've done lately, and I know they've been the wrong things to do.

Not listening to what Mom and Dad wanted me to do was wrong. Blaming Crystal and Mary Ann when things got out of hand was wrong. And not stopping Arielle and Danielle from doing something that I knew would upset Pamela was really wrong.

I look at Mom and shake my head no. "I know what I did was wrong," I say in a soft voice. I try to swallow, but when I do, I feel tears starting to form in the corners of my eyes. "I haven't been ten very long, and I already feel like I stink at it," I say to Mom and Dad.

Tears start to trickle down my face. Dad hands me a tissue, and I blow my nose into it.

"I think we've talked about this enough for now," says Dad. "Why don't you spend some time in your room thinking about what happened."

He bends down and kisses me on the forehead. But I can tell it's not an *I'm-so-happy-you're-my-daughter* kiss. It's more of an *I-love-you-because-you're-my-daughter-but-I-don't-like-what-you-did* kiss.

"I'm sure you're tired," says Mom. She pulls my comforter up over me. "Why don't you rest while you think."

Mom and Dad leave the room. I pull my covers up around my chin. I'm not sure if there's a word that means tired, sad, bad, upset, and disappointed in myself, but if there is, that's the word that would describe me.

And it's not at all how I want to describe myself.

NEW BEGINNINGS

I rub the soft fur behind Cheeseburger's ears.

When I turned eight, Grandma told me you get to make one wish for each year old that you are. Right now, I don't need to make ten wishes. I just need to make one.

I squeeze my eyes shut and pretend like I'm at the wish pond. *I wish I could restart being ten and do a good job of it.*

I keep my eyes closed and think about everything that happened.

When Mary Ann and I came up with the idea of having a sleepover, it seemed like such a good idea. I thought I would invite a few friends and plan some fun things.

Even when Mary Ann said we should make it the biggest, bestest sleepover ever, I never thought it would turn into the biggest, worstest sleepover ever.

I pull Cheeseburger in close to me. Mom and Dad were so nice about letting me have a sleepover. I feel like they did what I wanted them to do, but I didn't do what they wanted me to do, and just thinking about it makes me feel terrible.

Mom and Dad were right. I didn't think through the consequences of my actions. I shouldn't have listened to what my friends had to say. I should have done what I knew was right. I think about my wish. I really do wish I could start over being ten and do a good job of it. Then it hits me. I can't start over, but I can do a good job of it . . . starting now!

I pull back my covers and hop out of bed. I have a plan.

I quickly put on some clothes and throw my hair into a ponytail. Then I sit down at my desk. "Cheeseburger, I've got a lot of work to do and I want to do a good job doing it," I say to my cat.

I get out markers, scissors, construction paper, a plain T-shirt, one of my leftover party favors, some old photos, and some glue.

I cut and glue and color. I use my neatest writing and think carefully about what I'm making. When I'm done, I gather up everything that I made and put it into a shopping bag.

Time to put my plan into place.

Step 1: I go into the kitchen to talk to Mom and Dad.

"Mallory, why aren't you resting?" asks Mom.

"I can't rest when I have things to do," I tell my parents. I reach into my shopping bag and pull out the apology card I made for Mom and Dad. I watch while they read it.

"I want you to know how sorry I am about everything that happened at the sleepover," I tell my parents.

Mom and Dad look at each other. "Mallory, as long as you understand what you did wrong and promise us that you won't let something like that happen again, we don't need to dwell on it," says Dad.

"I'm glad you feel that way," I say to Dad. "Because I've got some other people I need to see."

Step 2: I get into the minivan with Mom.

When we get to Crystal's house, Mom pulls the minivan to a stop. "Wait for me," I say.

Mom smiles. "I'm not going anywhere."

But I am. I walk up to Crystal's house and ring the bell. A minute later, someone opens the door and it's Crystal.

She frowns when she sees me. "Mallory, what are you doing here?"

I clear my throat and start talking. "I want to apologize for how I acted and what I said about you at the party. I should have gone outside and gotten you when everyone started making a mess." I hold up the *World's Best Babysitter* T-shirt that I made for Crystal. "I hope you'll forgive me, and I really hope you'll keep being my babysitter."

Crystal's frown turns into a smile. She takes the T-shirt and slips it on over her clothes. Then she gives me a big hug.

"You know I have a soft spot for T-shirts," she says with a smile.

I'm glad she likes her gift. I hug Crystal and wave good-bye. There's someone else I need to go see.

When Mom and I pull up in front of Pamela's house, I hop out of the minivan. "This might take a little longer," I tell Mom.

She nods like she understands.

I clutch the shopping bag in my hand as I walk up the sidewalk. I know this won't be easy. Pamela was really upset when she left. I take a deep breath and ring the doorbell.

When the door opens, Pamela is standing on the other side.

"If you came to bring me my party favor, I still don't want it," says Pamela.

I shake my head. "What I came to bring you was an apology and an explanation."

Pamela is quiet like she's listening.

"I want you to know how sorry I am about everything that happened at the sleepover. It was Arielle and Danielle's idea to draw on you. It was their fault for starting it, but it was my fault for not stopping it. I knew you wouldn't think it was funny."

Pamela is quiet. I can't tell if she's accepting my apology or not.

"Pamela, I'm really, really, really sorry about what happened."

Pamela knows when I say something three times, I really mean it, but she still doesn't say anything.

I reach into my shopping bag and pull out a marker. "If you don't believe me that I'm truly sorry, I'll write *I'm sorry* all over my arms and face."

I didn't mean to be funny, but Pamela actually laughs when I say that.

"Mallory, don't be silly. I don't want you to write on yourself."

I can tell Pamela just accepted my apology. I lean over and give her a big hug, and she hugs me back. Then I leave. Time to put the next part of my plan into place.

Step 3: When Mom and I drive by the Winstons' house, I ask her to drop me off. I walk up to their house and ring the bell.

Too bad for me, Winnie is the one who answers the door. She was the last person I wanted to see. "May I speak to Mary Ann please?"

Winnie shakes her head. "I never thought I'd say this, but I don't think Mary Ann wants to speak to you."

Sometimes I listen to Winnie, and sometimes I don't, and now is one of those times when I don't.

I push past Winnie and walk straight to Mary Ann's room. She is lying down on her bed. I know she's upset about what I said to her last night. I sit down beside her.

"Do you remember last year in third grade when Mrs. Daily taught us the expression *setting the record straight*?"

Mary Ann doesn't nod like she remembers, but I know she does. I keep talking. "Well, I need to set the record straight."

Mary Ann sits up a little, like she's starting to listen.

"I blamed you for some things that weren't your fault. It wasn't your fault that you told me that a bigger party would be more fun. I should have listened to my parents when they said they wanted to keep it small. I shouldn't have blamed you for leaving the kitchen a mess and going to make water balloons. I should have gone to get Crystal when the problems started. And I shouldn't have blamed you for laughing when Arielle and Danielle were decorating Pamela. I knew she wouldn't think it was funny, and I should have stopped them."

I pause like it is Mary Ann's turn to say something, and she does.

"Mallory, I'm sorry too. I'm your best friend, and lately, I don't think I've been acting like a very good one."

I didn't expect Mary Ann to apologize, but it makes me feel good that she did. I guess we both did things that were wrong and we know it.

I hold up my pinkie. "Let's pinkie swear that we'll always try to be the best, best friends."

Mary Ann giggles and hooks her pinkie around mine. "Best, best, best friends," she says.

Then I remember what I brought for Mary Ann. I take one of the party favors we made out of the bag. "I put a picture of our first sleepover in it," I say. "I hope you like it."

Mary Ann looks at the picture of us in our pajamas when we were little. "We've been having sleepovers for a long time," she says.

"And I hope we keep having them for a long, long, long time," I say.

We hug each other. Then we talk for a few minutes about the party, especially the fun parts, and then I go home.

When I get to my room, I collapse on my bed. I'm not sure if it was last night's or this morning's activities or both, but something is making me very sleepy.

I rub Cheeseburger's back and feel her body relax next to mine. I can tell they all liked what I made them, and even better, they liked my apologies. It feels a lot better doing things the right way than the wrong way. I take a deep breath. My eyelids are starting to feel heavy. I think for a minute. Then I realize there's one more step in my plan.

Step 4: I close my eyes.

BIRTHDAY MAGIC

I feel someone shaking my shoulder. "Mallory, time to wake up," I hear a voice say.

I open my eyes and look at the clock. Then I look again. It's six o'clock For a minute, I'm not even sure what day it is. Then I remember.

I must have fallen asleep when I got home from seeing Mary Ann and Pamela

and Crystal, and slept for the rest of
the day.

Mom looks at me and smiles. "I'm glad
to see the birthday girl is finally awake."

"Remember? It wasn't really my
birthday," I say.

Mom laughs. "That doesn't mean we
can't have a celebration."

I frown. Even though I apologized to
everyone and everyone accepted my
apology, I'm ready to put my birthday
behind me and start fresh.

Mom shakes her head like she can tell
what I'm thinking and doesn't agree with
it. She gives me an *I'm-the-mom-and-what-I-say-goes* look. "Come to the kitchen. We're
going to have dinner in a few minutes and
celebrate as a family. If it makes you feel
better, we can say it is your *un-birthday*
celebration."

I know there's no sense arguing with
Mom. And the truth is . . . it sounds like fun
to be the un-birthday girl. I sit up in bed.
"I'll be right there."

Mom laughs. "Take all the time you
need. Dinner can't start without you."

I smile and hop out of bed as Mom
leaves. For the first time today, I'm
starting to feel like celebrating.

I put a clip in my hair and scoop up Cheeseburger. "Time for my un-birthday dinner," I say out loud.

Everyone smiles when I walk into the kitchen.

I go straight to my seat, pick up my knife, and tap it against the side of my water glass. "I have something I'd like to say."

Max gives me an *I-hope-you're-not-going-to-make-a-long-annoying-speech-because-I-really-want-to-eat-dinner* look. But I ignore him. What I have to say won't take long, but it's important.

"Mom, Dad, before we start my celebration, I have a few things I want to say."

Mom and Dad sit down, like they're ready to listen.

I take a deep breath. I want my words to come out right.

"I know you and Dad gave me a special privilege, and you trusted me to follow certain rules. But I listened to my friends when I should have listened to you and I didn't stop them when they were doing the wrong thing. I'm really sorry about that."

Mom and Dad nod like they appreciate the apology.

"Mallory, we've already gone over this," says Dad.

"I know. But there's something else I want to say."

Max looks at his watch like it's time to eat, not talk, but I ignore him.

"I also want to say that I was so focused on thinking about how I was going to celebrate turning ten that I didn't really think about what it meant to be ten."

I pause so they can think about what I just said. Then I raise my right hand like

I'm making an official vow. "Now that I'm ten, I promise to act more grown up."

Mom and Dad smile.

"I really do promise to try to be more grown up," I tell Mom and Dad. "And I don't think it will be all that hard. I already feel older."

And I really do. Deep inside of me, I feel like I'm growing up by the minute.

"I'm really excited for a new decade," I say to Mom and Dad. "I'm ten, and then I'll be eleven, then twelve, and then I'll be a teenager. Soon I'll be wearing makeup and going to middle school and then high school and dating boys and driving a car and . . ."

Dad holds up his hand like it's a stop sign. "Not so fast," he says. "We want to spend some time enjoying ten-year-old Mallory."

"And we'd like to do that with your favorite dinner," says Mom. She places a big platter of spaghetti and meatballs on the table.

"It's about time!" says Max.

Yum! Mom knows how much I love this dinner. I fill every inch of my plate with noodles and sauce and top it off with three big meatballs.

Max looks at my plate like he's never seen so much pasta on one plate. "You'll never eat all that," says my brother.

I twirl a bunch of noodles around my fork and stick them in my mouth. "Now that I'm ten, I have a much bigger appetite," I say when I'm done chewing.

Everyone laughs, even Max. Mom and Dad and Max fill their plates with spaghetti and meatballs and start eating. There are lots of *mmms* and not much talking at the McDonald dinner table. I think my family likes my un-birthday dinner as much as I do.

Knowing everyone is happy makes me feel good and hungry! I take a big bite of a meatball. Then another bite of noodles. I eat until my plate is squeaky clean.

"I hope you saved some room for cake," says Mom. She carries a chocolate cake with pink roses to the table.

"Happy un-birthday, Mallory," say Dad and Max as Mom lights the candles on the cake. Even Champ barks and Cheeseburger purrs like they want to wish me a happy birthday too.

"Make a wish," says Dad.

"I wish for another sleepover," I say out loud.

Mom and Dad look at each other. "Mallory, that wish might not come true for a long time," says Dad.

I laugh. "Just kidding," I say to my parents. I think about the wish I made earlier. I wished I could restart being ten and do a good job of it.

"My wish already came true," I say. I smile and Mom snaps a picture of me.

I close my eyes. Then I think about what Grandma said about birthday magic. It is starting to make sense. What I really wanted was exactly what I got.

I open my eyes and blow out my candles. Mom gives me a big hug.

Dad rumples my hair. "Sweet Potato, I hope your wish comes true."

I reach up and wrap my arms around Dad. "My wish already came true," I tell Dad. "Like magic."

MALLORY'S SLEEPOVER CHECKLIST

☐ *The list.* Put together a list of everyone you want to invite.

☐ *The invitations.* Everyone loves getting an invitation. You can buy them, make them, or send them from the computer.

☐ *The schedule.* Lots can happen at a sleepover. Make a schedule and stick to it.

☐ *Things to do.* You can play games, watch movies, bake, and even have a campfire in your backyard.

☐ *Things to eat.* Sleepovers make everyone hungry! Make sure you have lots of good party food. Just follow the G.G.P.C.C. rule. That's short for Goldfish, gummies, pretzels, popcorn, candy, and cookies. Mmmm!

☐ *Pajamas, pillows, and sleeping bags.* Don't forget to tell your friends to bring their own. (Toothbrushes optional!)

☐ *Scary stories.* Almost everyone loves scary stories, but not too scary!

☐ *Surprises.* Everyone loves surprises!!! Just make sure they are good surprises!

☐ *The cake.* You can't have a party without a cake.

☐ *Party favors.* Not necessary, but nice. And here's the best part: you can have fun making them yourself!

I think that covers it. You now know everything you need to start planning a super sleepover. The only thing left to do is to have fun!

A SCRAPBOOK

Here's something I never thought I would say: I'm glad my birthday celebration is over.

Don't get me wrong — there are parts of my sleepover that I never want to forget. But there are also some parts that I'm sure I'll always remember, even though part of me would much rather forget them.

Mary Ann made me a scrapbook from the party, and here's the good news: she only put in pictures that fall into the *things-I-want-to-remember* category.

I hope you enjoy looking at these pictures as much as I did!

Here's my favorite picture. Mary Ann and me in our matching cupcake pajamas. We made a pinkie swear to wear them every year on both of our birthdays, no matter how big we get.

Here's a picture of me with all my friends at my party.

Here's a picture of me opening my presents.

Last but not least is my favorite picture . . . me blowing out my birthday candles or I guess I should say, my un-birthday candles. Mary Ann got this picture from Mom.

The good news is that I got what I wished for. As Grandma would say, it was birthday magic.

I'm making one last wish, and I really want it to come true, so hopefully it will.

I wish that when your birthday rolls around, a little magic falls your way and all of your wishes come true!

Big, huge hugs and kisses,

Mallory

(a.k.a. the birthday fairy)

Darby Creek
A division of Lerner Publishing Group, Inc.
241 First Avenue North
Minneapolis, MN 55401 U.S.A.

website address: www.lernerbooks.com

The images in this book are used with the permission of: Cover background: © iStockphoto.com/Chuck Schmidt, © iStockphoto.com/sinankocaslan (pillow).

Main body text set in LuMarcLL 14/20. Typeface provided by Linotype.

Library of Congress Cataloging-in-Publication Data

Friedman, Laurie B.
    Mallory's Super Sleepover / by Laurie Friedman ; illustrations by Jennifer Kalis.
        p.   cm. — (Mallory ; #16)
    Summary: When Mallory plans a sleepover to celebrate her tenth birthday, she has a hard time pleasing both her friends and her parents.
    ISBN: 978-0-8225-8887-0 (trade hardcover : alk. paper) [1. Sleepovers—Fiction. 2. Parties—Fiction. 3. Birthdays—Fiction. 4. Behavior—Fiction.]
    I. Kalis, Jennifer, ill. II. Title.
    PZ7.F89773Mau 2011
    [Fic]—dc22   2010044418

Manufactured in the United States of America
2 — SB — 7/15/12